Rise & Shine

A Challah-Day Tale

To my mother-in-law, Gertrude Ostrove, who is just TERRIFIC and to my
"well-bread" grandchildren, Jakey and Sophie – K.O.

To "The Girls" who love to bake. – K.S.

KAR-BEN Publishing
A division of Lerner Publishing Group, Inc.
241 First Avenue North
Minneapolis, MN 55401 U.S.A.
800-4KARBEN

Website address: www.karben.com

Library of Congress Cataloging-in-Publication Data

Ostrove, Karen.
    Rise & Shine : A Challah-Day Tale / by Karen Ostrove ; illustrated by
Kimberley Scott.
       p.   cm.
    Summary: When Sammy and Sophie find an old paper with strange
writing they take it to Shalom House, where their grandmother and
other seniors recognize it as a recipe in Yiddish, and all pitch in to bake
challah.
    ISBN 978–0–7613–7499–2 (lib. bdg. : alk. paper)
    [1. Stories in rhyme. 2. Challah (Bread)—Fiction. 3. Bread—Fiction.
4. Baking—Fiction. 5. Grandmothers—Fiction. 6. Jews—United States—
Fiction.] I. Scott, Kimberley, ill. II. Title. III. Title: Rise and shine.
PZ8.3.O08228Ris 2013
[E]—dc23   2012009499

Manufactured in the United States of America
1 – PC – 12/31/12

Rise & Shine

A Challah-Day Tale

by Karen Ostrove   illustrated by Kimberley Scott

KAR-BEN
PUBLISHING

Sammy and Sophie were spending the day
Up in the attic, a fun place to play.

As Sophie tried on an old apron she found
A crumpled up paper that fell to the ground.

"What are these letters? Hey, what does it say?"
Sophie tried turning it every which way.
"It looks like a language from long, long ago.
Let's show Grandma Gert; I am sure she will know."

TALES OF THE

WORLD HISTO

Sweet Grandma Gert and her sister Aunt Jenny
Live at Shalom House with Great Uncle Benny,
And a crusty old fellow called Grumpy Old Ned
Who won't ever smile. He just grumbles instead.

Schedule

"Where is our grandma?" they asked at the door.
"It's exercise day, so she's on the third floor."

Grandma and Jenny were bending and stretching.

Benny was clapping, and Old Ned was kvetching.

"Grandma Gert, here's a mystery, please take a look.
We've never seen writing like this in a book."
"The writing is Yiddish—and this is my guess—
It's a recipe written by MY Grandma Bess."

The group gathered 'round and agreed that they could
Read the old Yiddish and soon understood
The directions, and, clutching the paper they ran
Into the kitchen, to find a big pan.

Grandma Gert's glasses were perched on her nose.
She opened the cupboards and carefully chose:

FLOUR

"Flour, my darlings, just fill this bowl up.
Put in some water; it needs a full cup."

Benny was watching and quick to advise,
"Yeast goes in next; it will make this thing rise."

Eggs and then oil were checked off the list
They re-read the recipe; nothing was missed.

"Punch it and knead it," said Grumpy Old Ned,
"Then roll it and braid it! It's *challah*; it's bread!"

Everyone braided with three strands or four.
Sophie and Sammy tried braiding with more!

"Brush on a glaze, because this challah needs
A finishing sprinkle of sesame seeds."

Cleaning the kitchen, they made it crumb-free.
The challah was baking while Grandma made tea.
"Just for Shabbat, we made challah so fine,
Perfect with candles and grape juice or wine."

Even Grumpy Old Ned broke out in a grin.
A bubble of laughter burst out from within.

"Come back next week to make more bread," he pleaded.
"Your CHALLAH-DAY visit was just what I KNEADED."

Bread Machine Challah

¼ c. oil
¾ c. water
2 eggs (save a tablespoon for glaze)
1 tsp. salt
¼ c. sugar
4 c. flour
1 package quick rise yeast

Place ingredients in bread machine in the order listed. Set to "dough". When ready, remove from machine. *Oil hands and knead a bit. Divide in two, and divide each half into three (or more) sections to braid. Place on cookie sheet. Cover lightly with plastic wrap and let rise until doubled. Mix saved egg with 1 Tbsp. water and brush on top. Add seeds if desired. Bake at 350 degrees for 20-25 minutes until brown.

Challah by hand

Mix the yeast, water, and sugar in a bowl and let bubble. Add rest of ingredients and knead until smooth. Place in oiled bowl, cover, and let rise until doubled in size (about 1 hour). Punch down and proceed from * above.